At Grandma's House

by Laura Verderosa

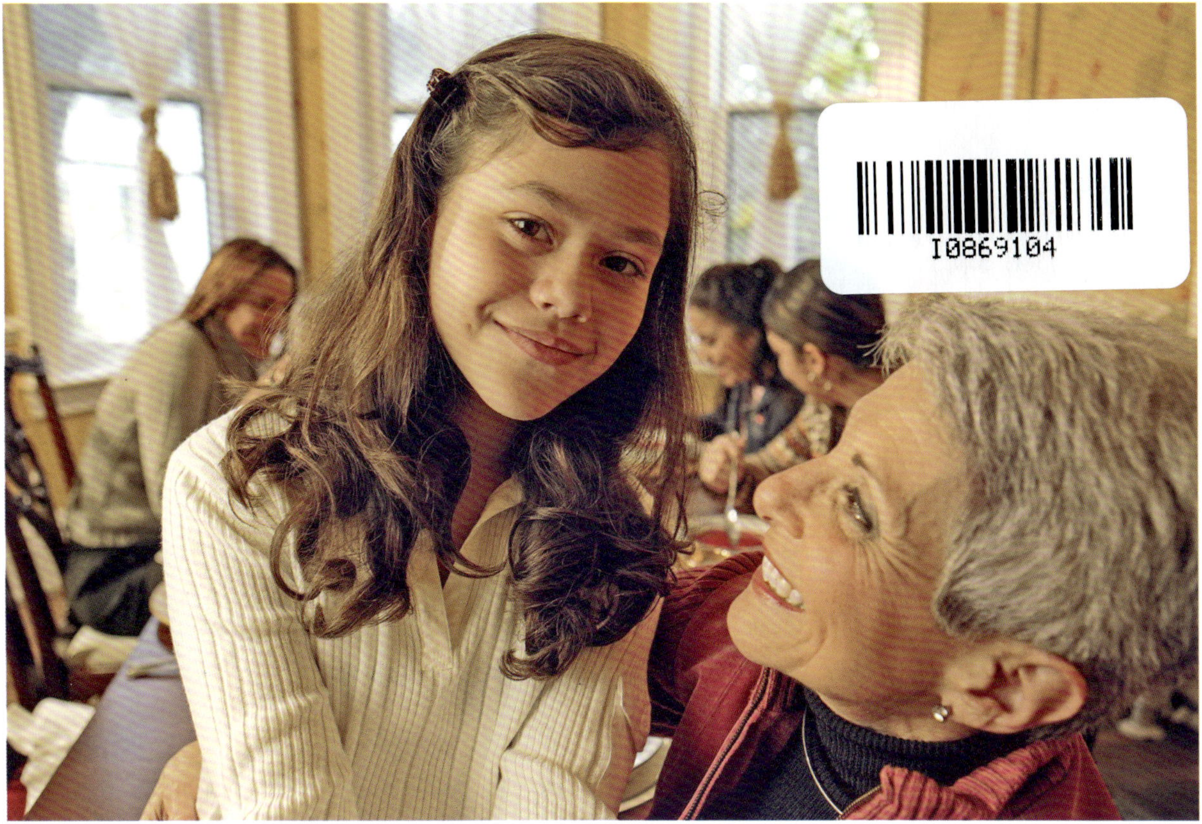

Picture Words

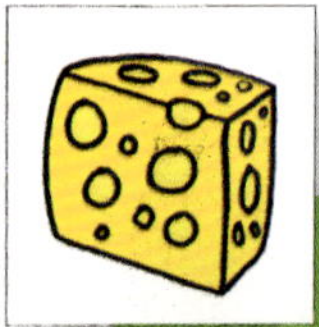

cheese

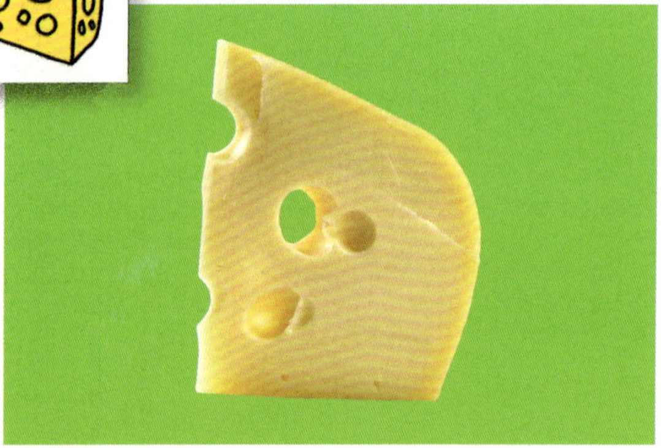

fruit

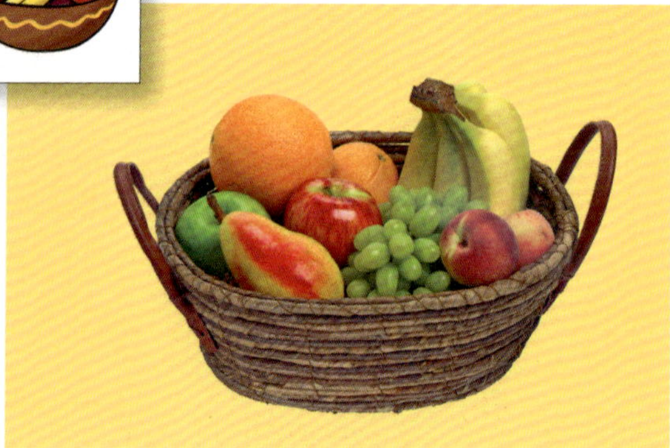

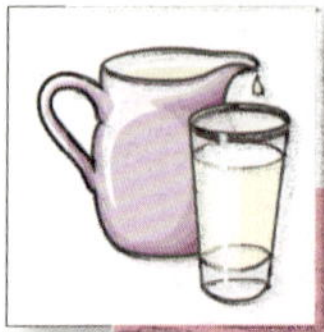

milk

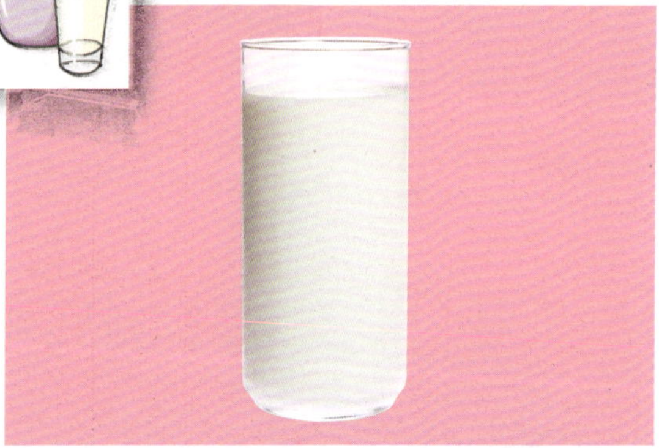

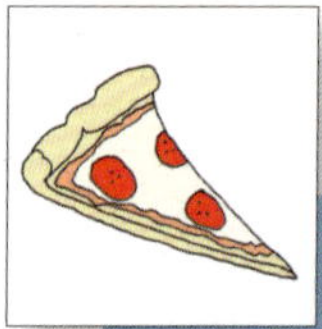

pizza

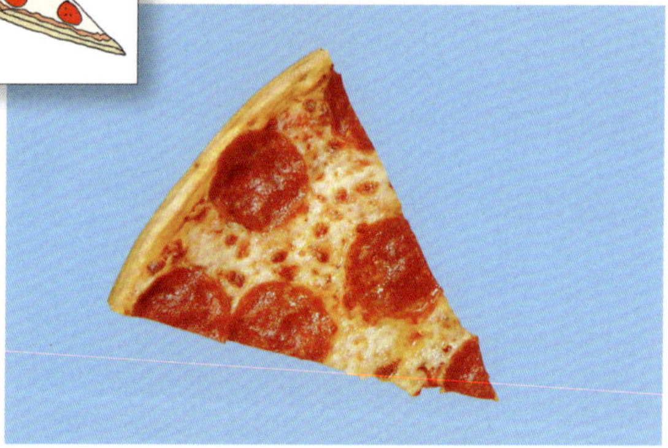

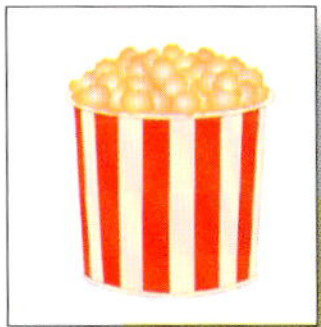

popcorn

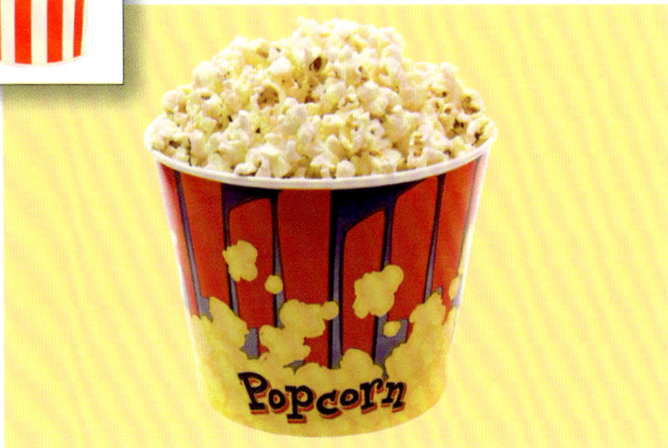

Sight Words

had

we

We had 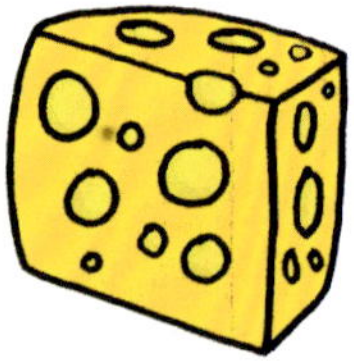 .

cheese

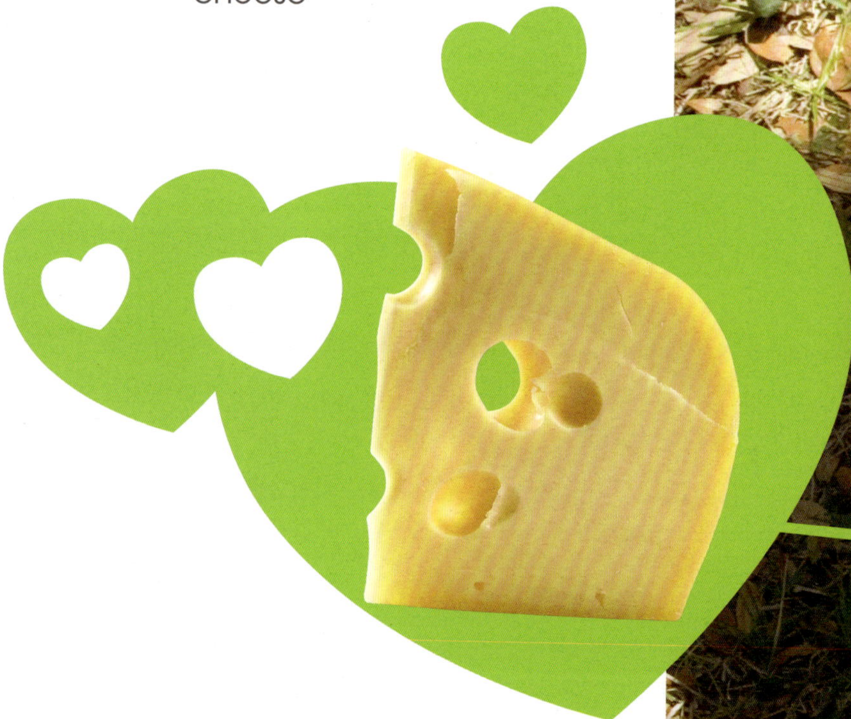

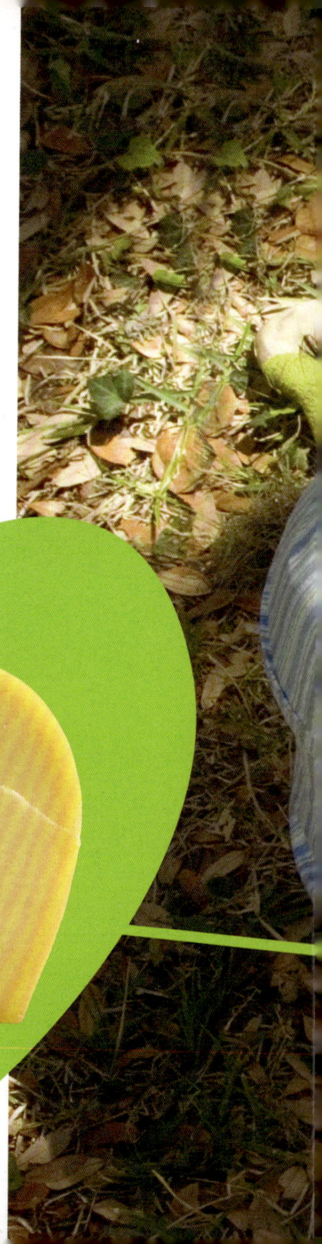

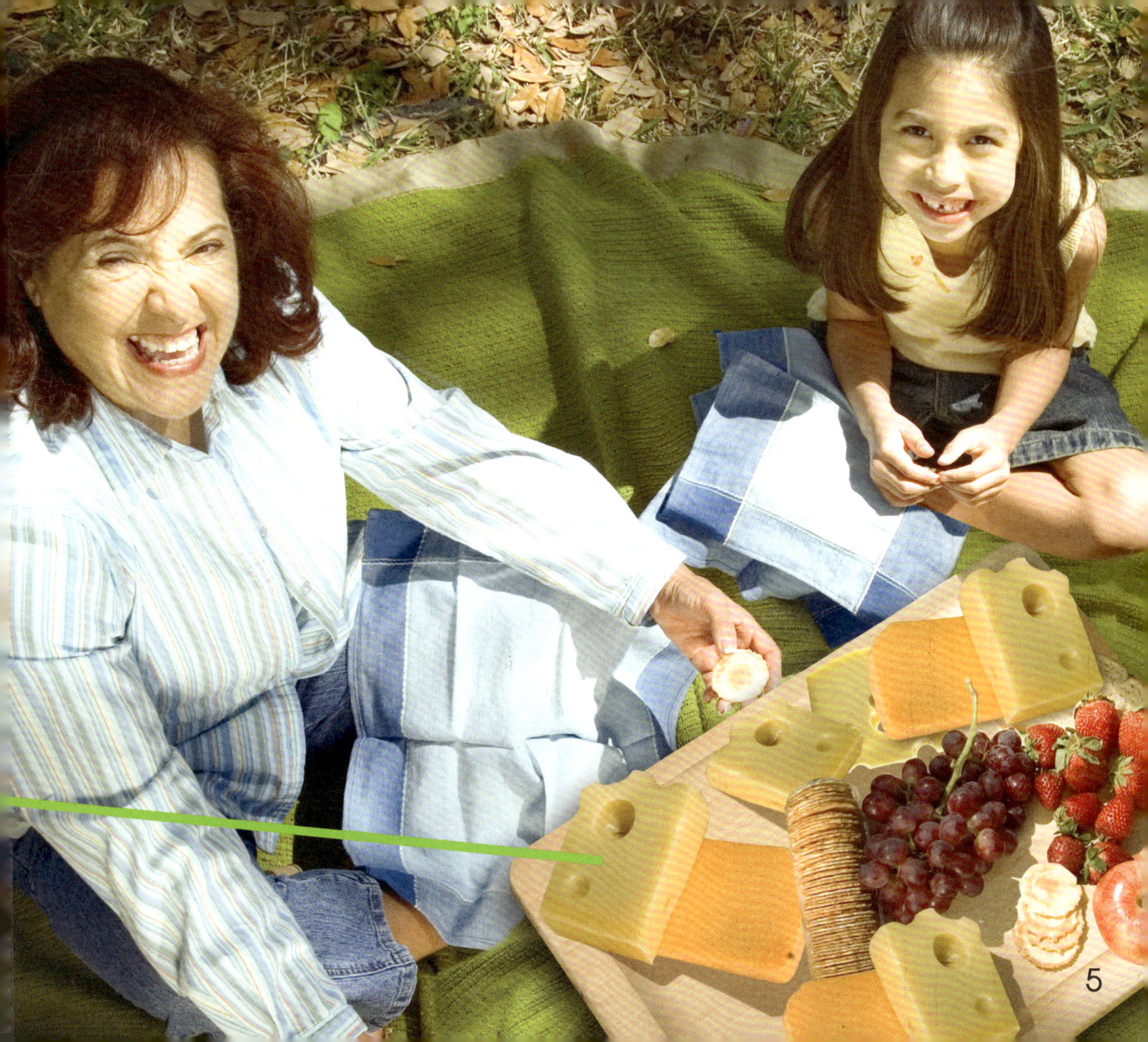

We had 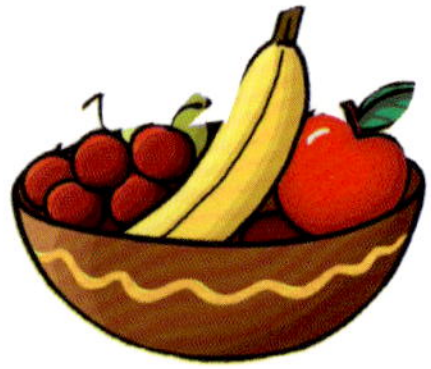 .

fruit

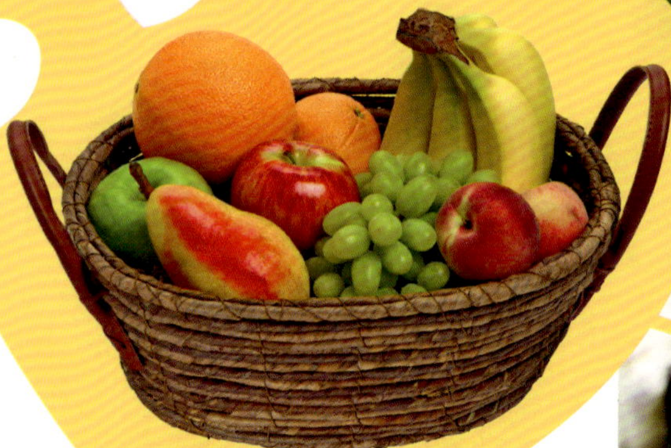

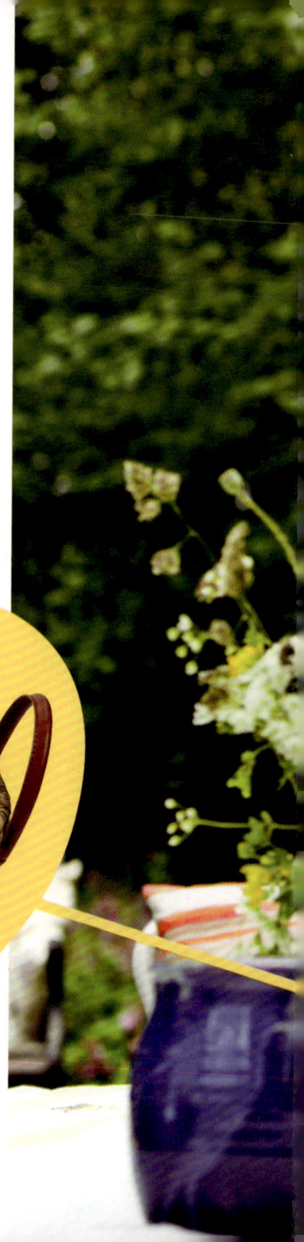

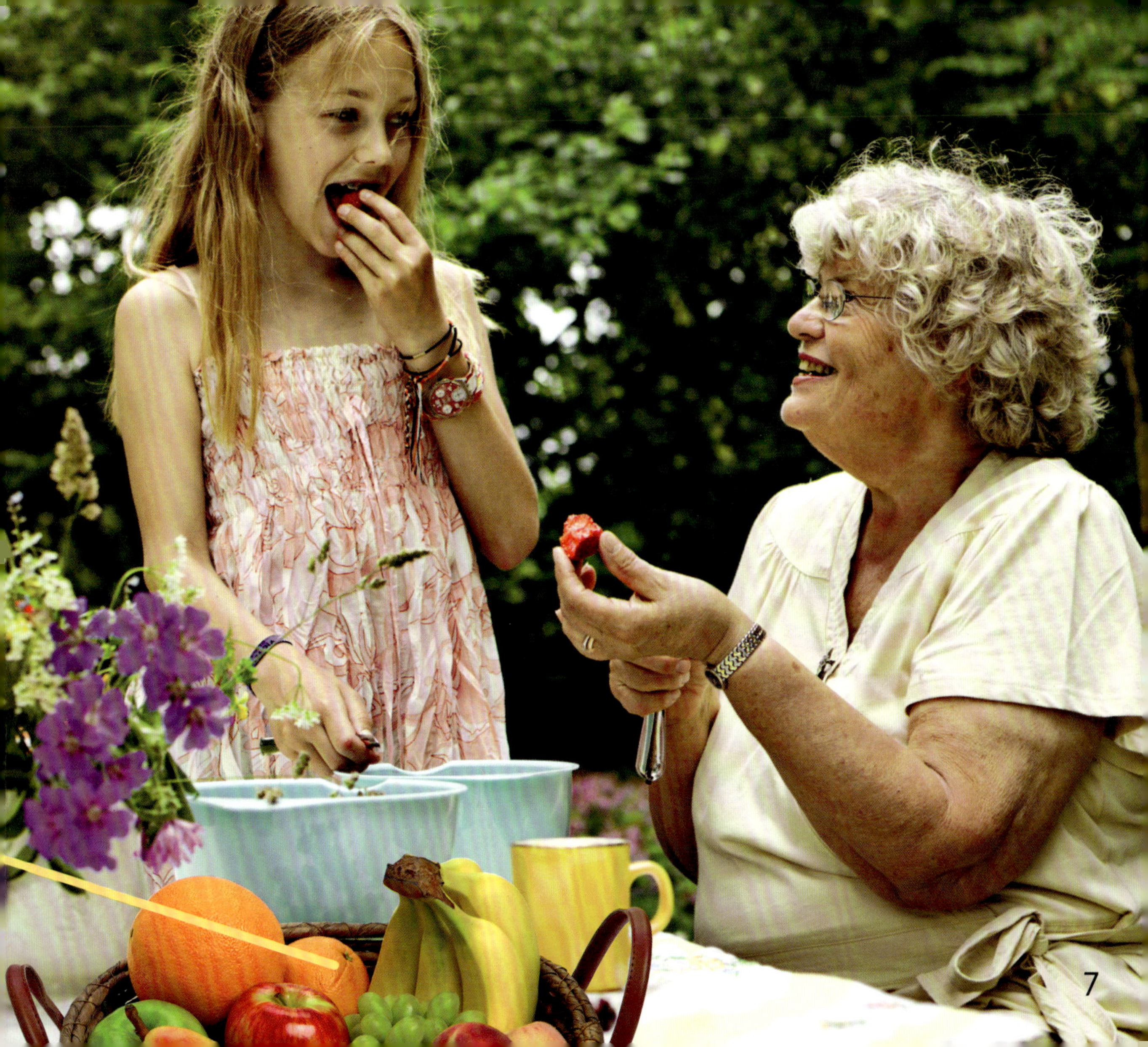

We had 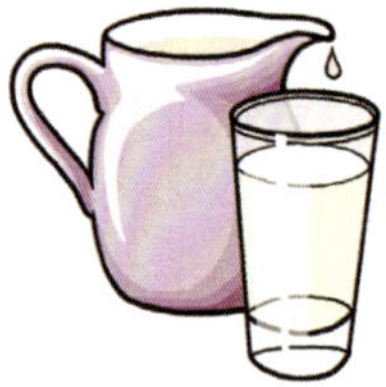 .

milk

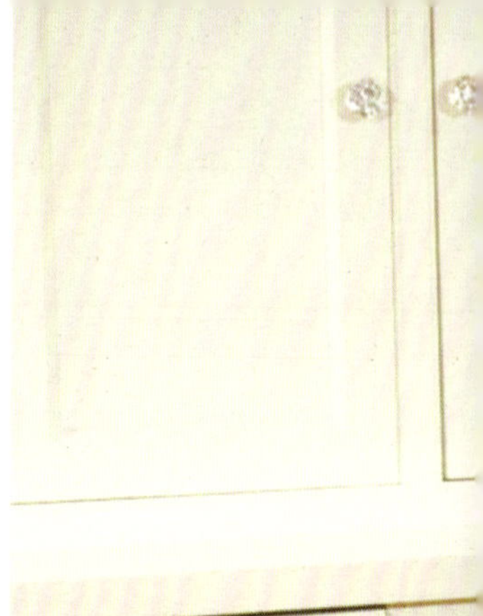

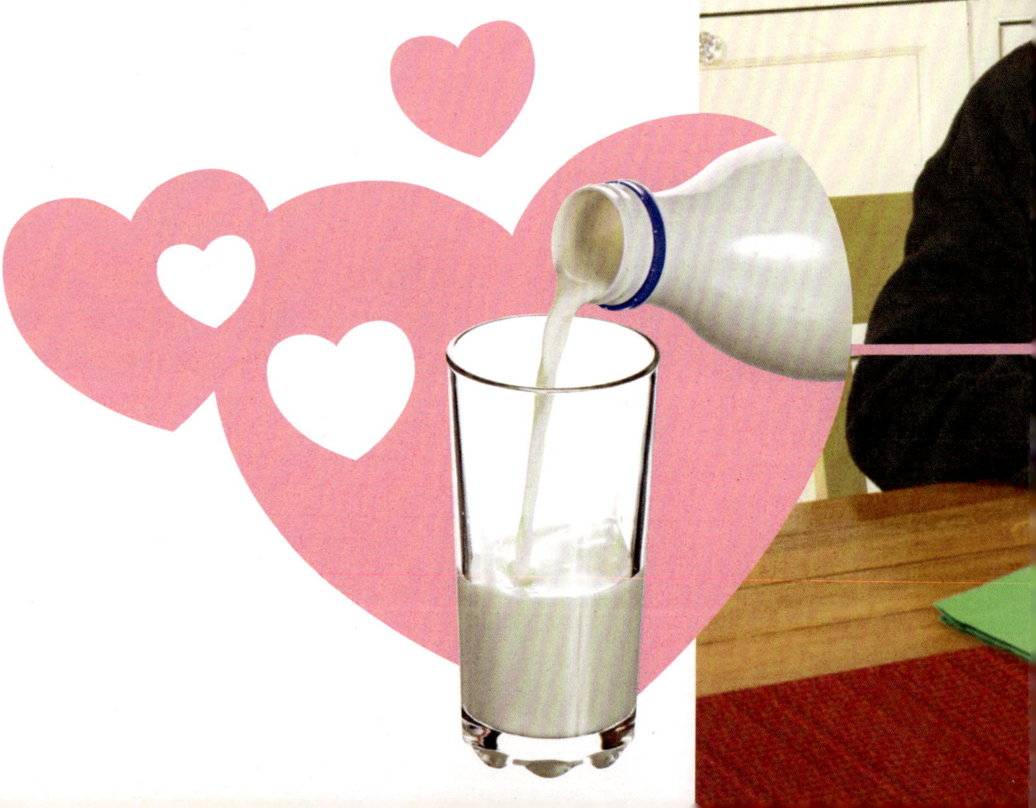

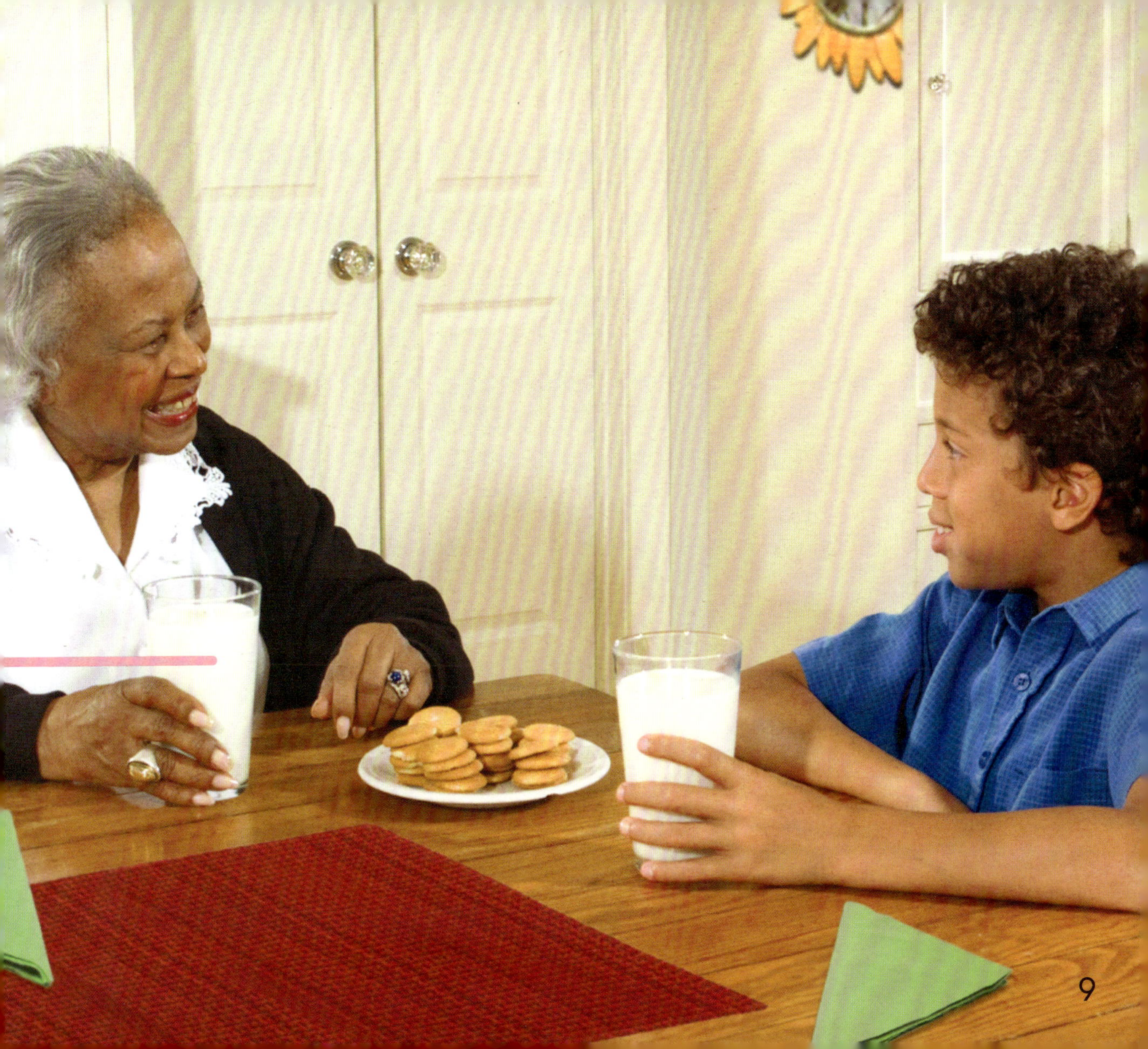

We had 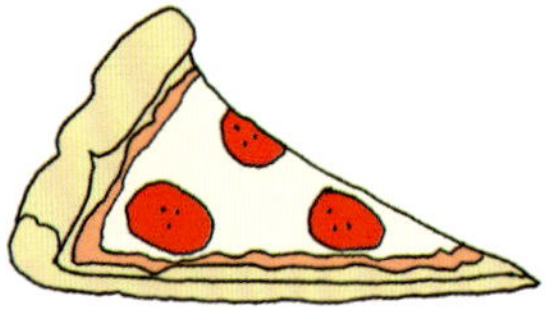 .

pizza

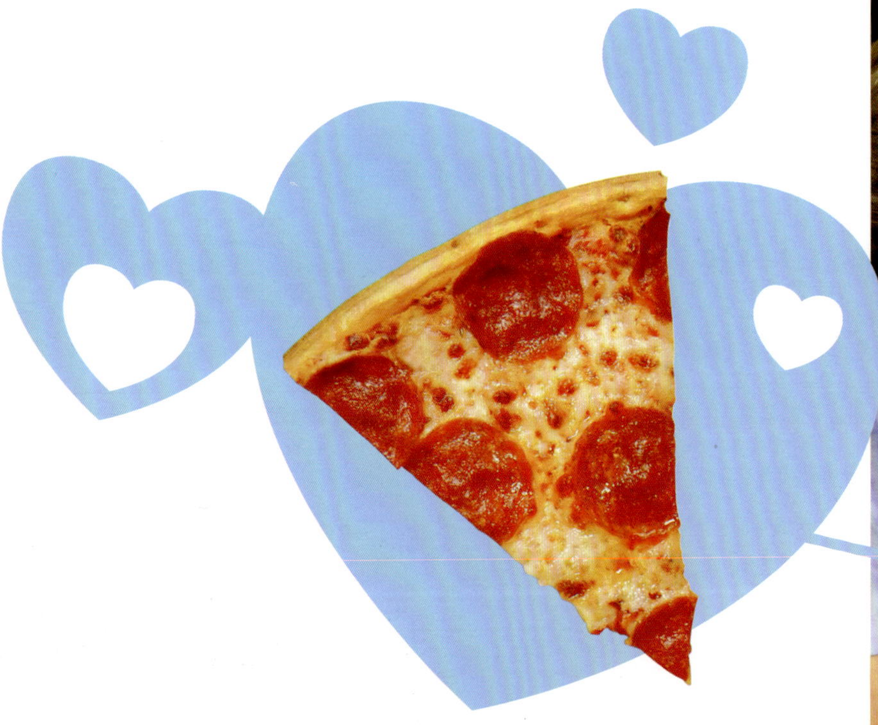

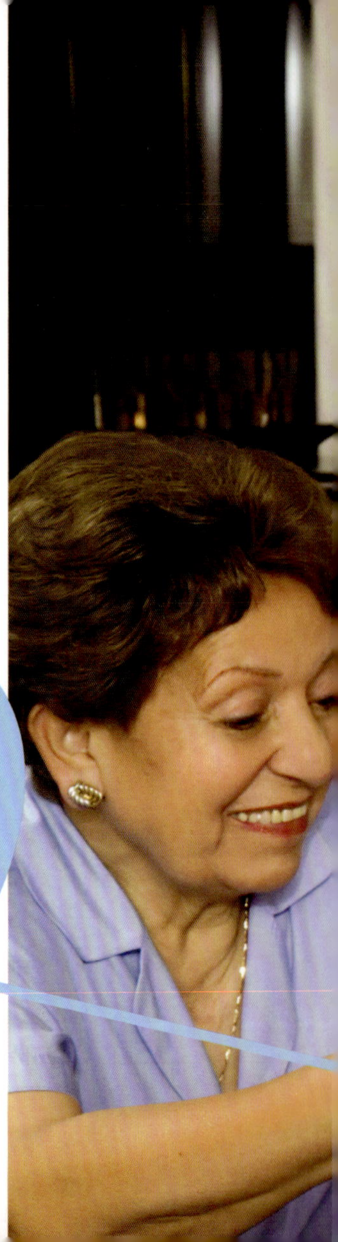

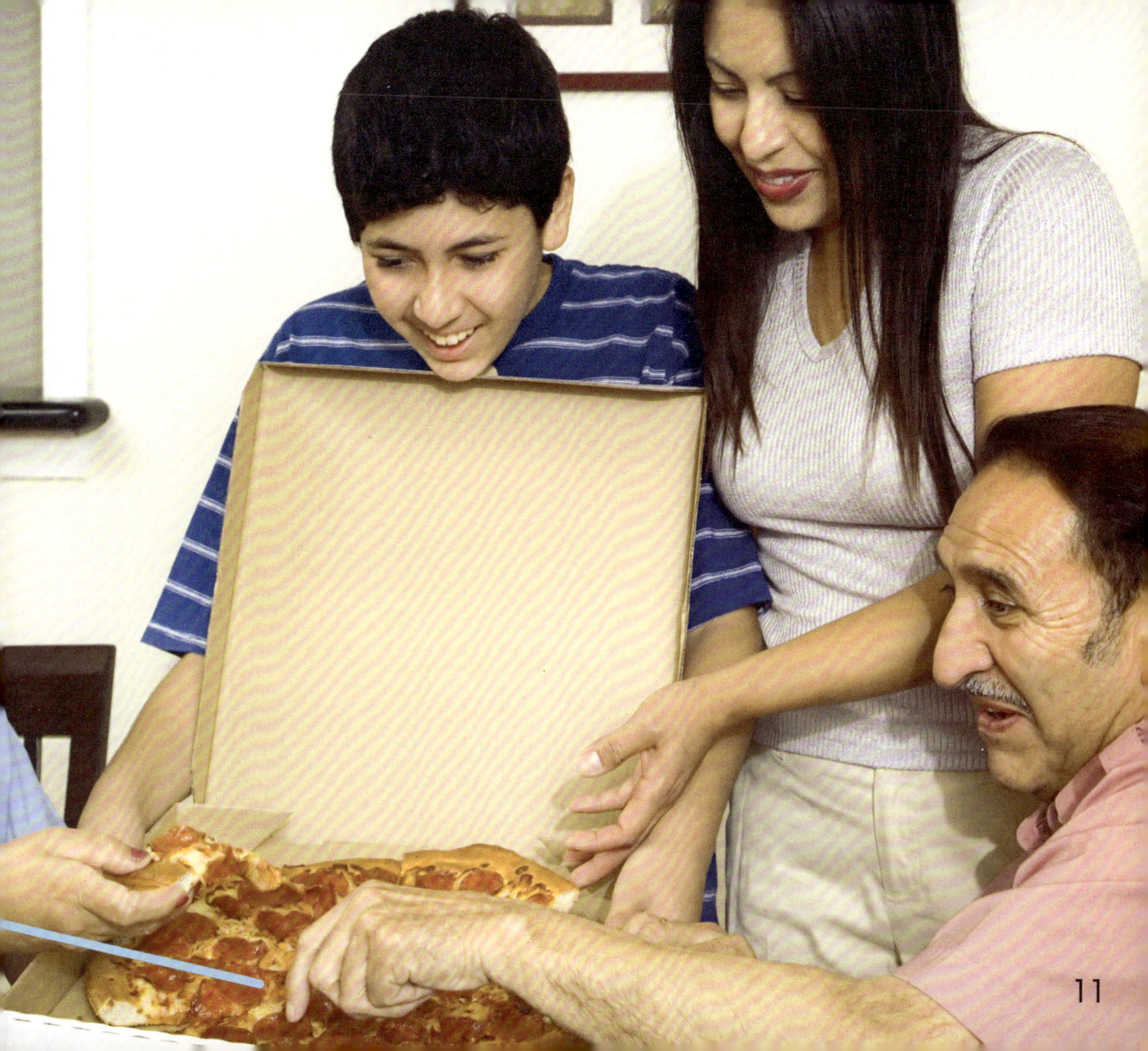

We had 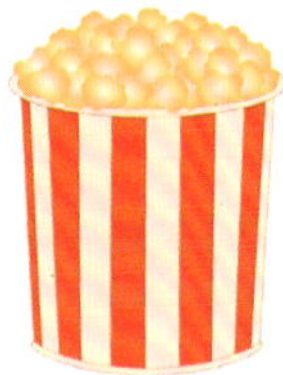 .

popcorn

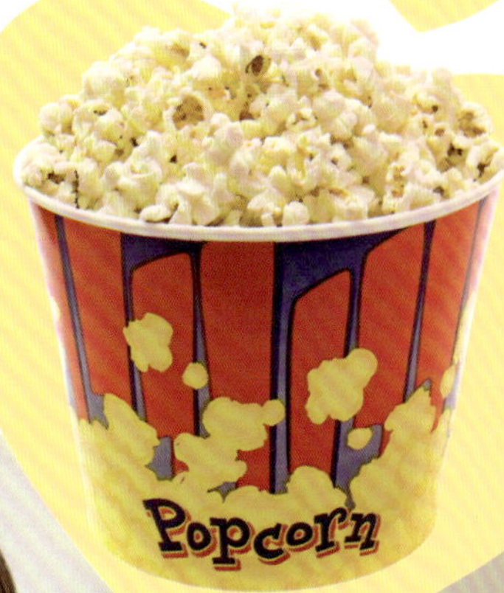

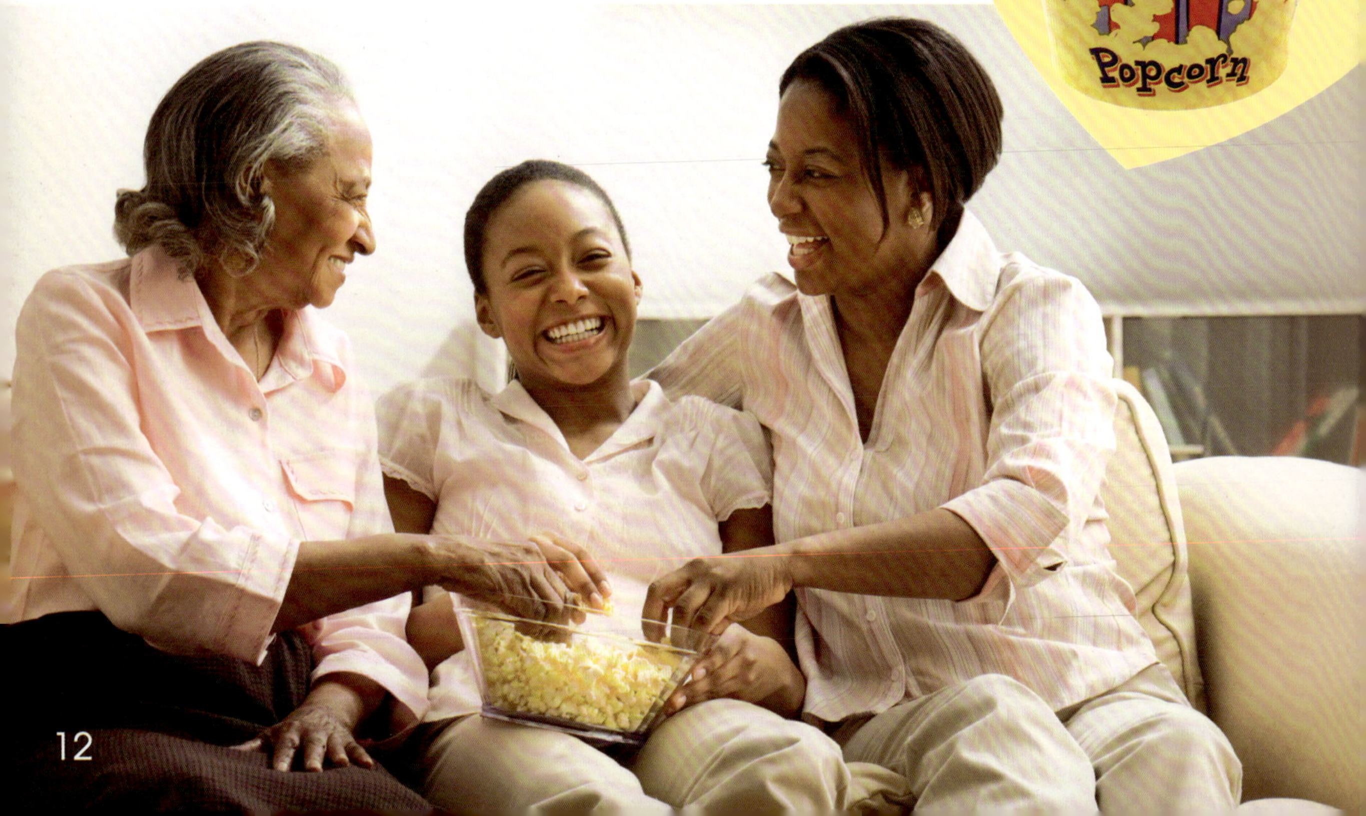